FOLK

poems about people

edited by
Robert Fisher

illustrated by
Penny Dann

ff

faber and faber
LONDON · BOSTON

First published in 1986
by Faber Limited
3 Queen Square London WC1N 3AU
This paperback edition first published in 1991

Photoset by Parker Typesetting Service, Leicester
Printed in England by Clays Ltd, St Ives plc
All rights reserved

A CIP record for this book is available
from the British Library

ISBN 0-571-16214-2

Contents

Acknowledgements

The editor is grateful for permission to use the following copyright material:

'Emma Hackett's Newsbook' by Allan Ahlberg from Allan Ahlberg: *Please Mrs Butler* (Kestrel Books 1983) pp. 18–19 Copyright © 1983 by Allan Ahlberg.

'My Sister Clarissa' and 'The Rev Arbuthnot-Armitage-Brown' from *To Aylsham Fair* by George Barker, reprinted by permission of Faber and Faber Ltd.

'Henry King' from *Cautionary Verses* by Hilaire Belloc, published by Gerald Duckworth & Co. Ltd.

'Night Starvation' and 'The Plughole Man' from *Bananas in Pyjamas* by Carey Blyton, reprinted by permission of Faber and Faber Ltd.

'Old Mrs Thing-um-e-bob' from *Figgie Hobbin* and 'Tom Bone' from *Collected Poems* by Charles Causley, published by Macmillan.

'There was a Man' from *Stranger than Unicorns* by Leonard Clark, published by Dobson Books Ltd.

'My Name Is . . .' from *Silver Bells and Cockleshells* by Pauline Clarke. Copyright © 1962 by Pauline Clarke, reproduced by permission of Curtis Brown Ltd, London.

'Miss T.' by Walter de la Mare, reprinted by permission of The Literary Trustees of Walter de la Mare and The Society of Authors as their representative.

'Herbaceous Plodd' by Michael Dugan from his *My Old Dad and Other Funny Things like Him*, Longman Cheshire, Melbourne, 1976.

'Oh Erica, Not Again!' and 'Be Quiet' by Max Fatchen from Max Fatchen: *Songs for My Dog & Other People* (Kestrel Books 1980) pp. 49, 52–53. Copyright © 1980 by Max Fatchen.

'Alone in the Grange' by Gregory Harrison, copyright ©, reprinted from *The Night of the Wild Horses*, published by Oxford University Press.

'Chester's Undoing' by Julie Holder, reprinted by permission of the author.

'My Brother Bert' and 'My Uncle Dan' from *Meet My Folks* by Ted Hughes, reprinted by permission of Faber and Faber Ltd.

7

'My Sister' from *Nonstop Nonsense* by Margaret Mahy, published by J. M. Dent & Sons Ltd.

'Cousin Reggie' and 'Cousin Nell' from *Sporting Relations* by Roger McGough, published by Eyre Methuen. Reprinted by permission of A. D. Peters & Co. Ltd.

'Granny' by Spike Milligan, reprinted by permission of Spike Milligan Productions Ltd.

'Bigtrousers Dan' by Peter Mortimer, reprinted by permission of Iron Press, from *Utter Nonsense* by Peter Mortimer, illustrated by Geoff Laws.

'The Cure' from *A Letter to Lucian* by Alfred Noyes, published by John Murray (Publishers) Ltd.

'The Man on the Flying Trapeze', reprinted by permission of Macmillan Publishing Company from *Circus!* by Jack Prelutsky. Text Copyright © 1974 by Jack Prelutsky.

'Mr Kartoffel' from *The Wandering Moon* by James Reeves, first published by William Heinemann Ltd in 1950, reprinted by permission of William Heinemann Ltd.

'My Singing Aunt' by James Reeves © by James Reeves 1952, first published 1952 by Oxford University Press in *The Blackbird in the Lilac*. Permission granted by the author's estate.

'Giant Jojo' by Michael Rosen, reprinted by permission of the author.

'Big Gumbo' and 'Jittery Jim' excerpted from the book *Laughing Time* by William Jay Smith, copyright © 1953, 1955, 1956, 1957, 1959, 1968, 1974, 1977, 1980 by William Jay Smith. Reprinted by permission of Delacorte Press/Seymour Lawrence.

'Seumas Beg' by James Stephens, reprinted by permission of The Society of Authors on behalf of the copyright owner, Mrs Iris Wise.

'Elastic Jones' © Derek Stuart, from *A Second Poetry Book* (Oxford University Press), compiled by John L. Foster, reprinted by permission of the author.

'Cavendish McKellar' and 'Walter Spaggot' from *The Ombley-Gombley* by Peter Wesley Smith, reprinted with the permission of Angus & Robertson (UK) Ltd.

Acknowledgements are also made to the few copyright holders whom the editor has been unable to trace in spite of careful enquiry.

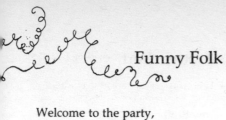

Funny Folk

Welcome to the party,
welcome to the fun,
the house is full of funny folk –
there's room for everyone!
meet . . .
my sister Clarissa (but don't try to kiss her!)
my big brother Bert, what's that in his shirt?
my mad Uncle Dan, he's a terrible man,
my Aunty who sings, my Granny with wings,
my friend Emma Hackett, oh what a racket!
There's Herbaceous Plod, he is rather odd,
and Elastic Jones, with his rubber bones,
poor Marjorie Fry (she's swallowed a fly!)
Here's young Henry King, still tongue-tied in string,
Big Gumbo, Giant Jojo,
Jittery Jim and Thin Flynn.
Mrs. Thing-um-e-bob came
with old . . . what's-his-name?
Who's that in the mirror, well riddle-me-ree,
everyone is different, that's plain to see,
(and who could be funnier than you, or me).
The gang's all here, oh what a din!
we're having a party

　　　　　　　　so come on in

　　　　　　　　　　　　　　Robert Fisher

My Brother Bert

Pets are the Hobby of my Brother Bert.
He used to go to school with a Mouse in his shirt.

His Hobby it grew, as some hobbies will,
And grew and GREW and GREW until –

Oh don't breathe a word, pretend you haven't heard.
A simply appalling thing has occurred –

The very thought makes me iller and iller:
Bert's brought home a gigantic Gorilla!

If you think that's really not such a scare,
What if it quarrels with his Grizzly Bear?

You still think you could keep your head?
What if the Lion from under the bed

And the four Ostriches that deposit
Their football eggs in his bedroom closet

And the Aardvark out of his bottom drawer
All danced out and joined in the Roar?

What if the Pangolins were to caper
Out of their nests behind the wallpaper?

With the fifty sorts of Bats
That hang on his hatstand like old hats,

And out of a shoebox the excitable Platypus
Along with the Ocelot or Jungle-Cattypus?

The Wombat, the Dingo, the Gecko, the Grampus –
How they would shake the house with their Rumpus!

Not to forget the Bandicoot
Who would certainly peer from his battered old boot.

Why it could be a dreadful day,
And what Oh what would the neighbours say!

Ted Hughes

Bigtrousers Dan

In the land of Rumplydoodle
where men eat jollips for tea,
and the cows in the hay
feel sleepy all day,
there's a wonderful sight to see.
On the banks of the River Bongbong,
in a hut made of turnips and cream,
sits a whiskery man,
name of Bigtrousers Dan,
and he plays with his brand new machine.
There are gronfles
and nogglets
and pluffles
and valves that go
ker-pling and ker-plang,
and a big sugar wheel
that revolves with a squeal
till it's oiled with a chocolate meringue.
There are wurdlies
and flumdings
and crumchies
that go round just as fast as they can,
and a big chocolate ball
that makes no sound at all,
thanks to clever old
Bigtrousers Dan.

Peter Mortimer

Cousin Nell

Cousin Nell
married a frogman
in the hope
that one day
he would turn into
a handsome prince.

Instead he turned into
a sewage pipe
near Gravesend
and was never seen again.

Roger McGough

Night Starvation or The Biter Bit

At night, my Uncle Rufus
(Or so I've heard it said)
Would put his teeth into a glass
Of water by his bed.

At three o'clock one morning
He woke up with a cough,
And as he reached out for his teeth –
They bit his hand right off.

Carey Blyton

My Sister Clarissa

My sister Clarissa spits twice if I kiss her
and once if I hold her hand.
I reprimand her – my name's Alexander –
for spitting I simply can't stand.

'Clarissa, Clarissa, my sister, is this a
really nice habit to practise?'
But she always replies with innocent eyes
rather softly, 'Dear Brother, the fact is

'I think I'm an ape with a very small grape
crushed to juice in my mastodon lips.
Since I am not a prude, though I hate being rude,
I am simply ejecting the pips.'

George Barker

My Uncle Dan

My Uncle Dan's an inventor, you may think
   that's very fine.
You may wish he was your Uncle instead of
   being mine –
If he wanted he could make a watch that bounces
   when it drops
He could make a helicopter out of string and
   bottle tops
Or any really useful thing you can't get in the
   shops.
   But Uncle Dan has other ideas:
   The bottomless glass for ginger beers,
   The toothless saw that's safe for the tree,
   A special word for a spelling bee
   (Like Lionocerangoutangadder),
   Or the roll-uppable rubber ladder,
   The mystery pie that bites when it's bit –
   My Uncle Dan invented it.

My Uncle Dan sits in his den inventing night and
   day.
His eyes peer from his hair and beard like mice
   from a load of hay.

And does he make the shoes that will go walks
   without your feet?
A shrinker to shrink instantly the elephants you
   meet?
A carver that just carves from the air steaks
   cooked and ready to eat?

No, no, he has other intentions –
Only perfectly useless inventions:
Glassless windows (they never break),
A medicine to cure the earthquake,
The unspillable screwed-down cup,
The stairs that go neither down nor up,
The door you simply paint on a wall –
Uncle Dan invented them all.

Ted Hughes

Emma Hackett's Newsbook

Last night my mum
Got really mad
And threw a jam tart
At my dad.
Dad lost his temper
Then with mother,
Threw one at her
And hit my brother.
My brother thought
It was my sister,
Threw two at her
But somehow missed her.
My sister,
She is only three,
Hurled four at him
And one at me!
I said I wouldn't
Stand for that,
Aimed one at her
And hit the cat.
The cat jumped up
Like he'd been shot,
And landed
In the baby's cot.
The baby –
Quietly sucking his thumb –
Then started howling
For my mum.

At which my mum
Got *really* mad,
And threw a Swiss roll
At my dad.

Allan Ahlberg

The Young Man of Devizes

There was a young man of Devizes,
Whose ears were of different sizes;
   One was quite small,
   And of no use at all,
But the other was huge and won prizes.

Anon

The Plug-hole Man

I know you're down there, Plug-hole Man,
 In the dark so utter,
For when I let the water out
 I hear you gasp and splutter.

And though I peer and peek and pry
 I've never seen you yet:
(I know you're down there, Plug-hole Man,
 In your home so wet).

But you will not be there for long
 For I've a *plan*, you see;
I'm going to catch you, Plug-hole Man,
 And Christian's helping me.

We'll fill the bath with water hot,
 Then give the plug a heave,
And rush down to the outside drain –
 And *catch* you as you leave!

Carey Blyton

Mr Kartoffel

Mr Kartoffel's a whimsical man;
He drinks his beer from a watering can,
And for no good reason that I can see
He fills his pockets with china tea.
He parts his hair with a knife and fork
And takes his ducks for a Sunday walk.
Says he, 'If my wife and I should choose
To wear our stockings outside our shoes,
Plant tulip bulbs in the baby's pram
And eat tobacco instead of jam
And fill the bath with cauliflowers,
That's nobody's business at all but ours.'
Says Mrs K., 'I may choose to travel
With a sack of grass or a sack of gravel,
Or paint my toes, one black, one white,
Or sit on a bird's nest half the night –
But whatever I do that is rum or rare,
I rather think that it's my affair.
So fill up your pockets with stamps and string,
And let us be ready for anything!'
Says Mr K. to his whimsical wife,
'How can we face the storms of life,
Unless we are ready for anything?
So if you've provided the stamps and string,
Let us pump up the saddle and harness the horse
And fill him with carrots and custard and sauce,
Let us leap on him lightly and give him a shove
And it's over the sea and away, my love!'

James Reeves

Chinese Sandmen

Chinese Sandmen,
Wise and creepy,
Croon dream-songs
To make us sleepy.
A Chinese maid with slanting eyes
Is queen of all their lullabies.
On her ancient moon-guitar
She strums a sleep-song to a star;
And when big China-shadows fall
Snow-white lilies hear her call.
Chinese Sandmen,
Wise and creepy,
Croon dream-songs
To make us sleepy.

Anon

Spring-heeled Jack

Spring-heeled Jack
Jumped up and down
Higher than anyone
Else in the town.

The heels of his boots
Were fitted with springs;
He could fly
Like a bird with wings.

The first time up
He jumped so high.
He made thunder
In the sky.

The second time up
He jumped far higher –
The North Wind set
His coat on fire.

The third time up
He jumped with zest –
The eagles plucked
His hair for a nest.

But the very last time
Spring-heeled Jack
Jumped to the moon
And never came back.

James K. Baxter

Elastic Jones

Elastic Jones had rubber bones.
He could bounce up and down like a ball.
When he was six, one of his tricks
Was jumping a ten-foot wall.

As the years went by, Elastic would try
To jump higher, and higher, and higher.
He amazed people by jumping a steeple,
Though he scratched his behind on the spire!

But, like many a star, he went too far,
Getting carried away with his power.
He boasted one day, 'Get out of my way,
I'm going to jump Blackpool Tower.'

He took off from near the end of the pier,
But he slipped and crashed into the top.
Amid cries and groans, Elastic Jones
Fell into the sea with a plop.

Derek Stuart

Tom Bone

My name is Tom Bone,
I live all alone
In a deep house on Winter Street.
  Through my mud wall
  The wolf-spiders crawl
  And the mole has his beat.

On my roof of green grass
All the day footsteps pass
In the heat and the cold,
  As snug in a bed
  With my name at its head
  One great secret I hold.

Tom Bone, when the owls rise
In the drifting night skies
Do you walk round about?
  All the solemn hours through
  I lie down just like you
  And sleep the night out.

Tom Bone, as you lie there
On your pillow of hair,
What grave thoughts do you keep?
  Tom says, Nonsense and stuff!
  You'll know soon enough.
  Sleep, darling, sleep.

Charles Causley

My Sister

My sister's remarkably light,
She can float to a fabulous height.
It's a troublesome thing,
But we tie her with string,
And we use her instead of a kite.

Margaret Mahy

The Old Codger of Broome

There was an old codger of Broome,
Who kept a baboon in his room.
  'It reminds me,' he said,
  'Of a friend who is dead.'
But he would never tell us of whom.

Anon

The Young Girl of Asturias

There was a young girl of Asturias,
Whose temper was frantic and furious.
  She used to throw eggs
  At her grandmother's legs –
A habit unpleasant, but curious.

Anon

Greedy Ned

A greedy young fellow named Ned
Ate up before going to bed –
  Six lobsters, one ham,
  Ten pickles with jam,
And when he woke up he was dead.

Anon

Betty

There once was a schoolgirl named Betty
Whose hair turned into spaghetti.
It gave her a fright,
Then she took a bite,
And ate it for lunch – and for tea!

Anon

Sir Nicketty Nox

Sir Nicketty Nox was an ancient knight,
So old was he that he'd lost his sight.
Blind as a mole, and slim as a fox,
And dry as a stick was Sir Nicketty Nox.

His sword and buckler were old and cracked,
So was his charger and that's a fact.
Thin as a rake from head to hocks,
Was this rickety nag of Sir Nicketty Nox.

A wife he had and daughters three,
And all were as old as old could be.
They mended the shirts and darned the socks
Of that old Antiquity, Nicketty Nox.

Sir Nicketty Nox would fly in a rage
If anyone tried to guess his age.
He'd mouth and mutter and tear his locks,
This very pernickety Nicketty Nox.

Hugh Chesterman

The Cure

'I've swallowed a fly,' cried Marjorie Fry.
   (We could hear it buzzing inside her.)
'And I haven't a hope of getting it out
   Unless I swallow a spider.'

We found a web by the garden wall,
   And back to the house we hurried
And offered the spider to Majorie Fry,
   Who was looking extremely worried.

'Now shut your eyelids, Marjorie Fry,
   And open your wee mouth wider.
Whatever it does, the fly won't buzz
   If only you'll swallow the spider.'

Alfred Noyes

Herbaceous Plodd

Herbaceous Plodd
is rather odd.
His eyes are red,
his nose is blue,
his neck and head
are joined by glue.
He only dines
on unripe peas,
bacon rinds
and melted cheese.
He rarely talks,
he never smiles,
but goes for walks
with crocodiles.

Michael Dugan

My Singing Aunt

The voice of magic melody
  With which my aunt delights me,
It drove my uncle to the grave
  And now his ghost affrights me.
This was the song she used to sing
  When I could scarcely prattle,
And as her top notes rose and fell
  They made the sideboard rattle:

'What makes a lady's cheeks so red,
  Her hair both long and wavy?
'Tis eating up her crusts of bread,
  Likewise her greens and gravy.
What makes the sailor tough and gay?
  What makes the ploughboy whistle?
'Tis eating salt-beef twice a day,
  And never mind the gristle.'

Thus sang my aunt in days gone by
  To soothe, caress, and calm me:
But what delighted me so much
  Drove her poor husband barmy.
So now when past the church I stray,
  'Tis not the night-wind moaning,
That chills my blood and stops my breath,
  But poor old uncle's groaning.

James Reeves

Henry King

Who chewed bits of String, and was early cut off in Dreadful Agonies.

The chief defect of Henry King
Was chewing little bits of String.
At last he swallowed some which tied
Itself in ugly Knots inside.

Physicians of the Utmost Fame
Were called at once; but when they came
They answered, as they took their Fees,
'There is no Cure for this Disease.
Henry will very soon be dead.'
His Parents stood about his Bed
Lamenting his Untimely Death,
When Henry, with his Latest Breath,
Cried, 'Oh, my Friends, be warned by me,
That Breakfast, Dinner, Lunch and Tea
Are all the Human Frame requires . . .'
With that the Wretched Child expires.

Hilaire Belloc

Chester's Undoing

Chester Lester Kirkenby Dale
Caught his sweater on a nail.
As Chester Lester started to travel
So his sweater began to unravel.
A great long trail of crinkly wool
Followed Chester down to school.
Then his ears unravelled!
His neck and his nose!
Chester undid from his head
To his toes.
Chester's undone, one un-purl, two un-plain,
Who's got the pattern to knit him again?

Julie Holder

38

The Reverend
Arbuthnot–Armitage–Brown

The Reverend Arbuthnot-Armitage-Brown
   stood up to deliver a Sermon.
He was not aware that a Whale was there
   accompanied by a Merman.

'I consider this world a terrible place,'
   he began. 'I consider the worm an
extremely unpleasant prospect to face.
   This is the text of my Sermon.'

But neither the Whale nor his friend could speak
   English or French or German
And so, though they heard, understood not a word
   of the Reverend Et Cetera's sermon.

For eighty-five hours by the Church clock
   he spoke about ashes and vermin
and ghouls and souls and burial holes
   and graves with a bone and a worm in.

Till 'Come,' said the Whale to his friend, whose name
   believe it or not, was Herman,
'This is no place for me. Let us go back to sea.
   Thank God I'm Whale and you're Merman.'

George Barker

Giant Jojo

I am Jojo
give me the sun to eat.
I am Jojo
give me the moon to suck.

The waters of my mouth
will put out the fires of the sun;
the waters of my mouth
will melt the light of the moon.

Day becomes night,
night becomes day.
I am Jojo
listen to what I say.

Michael Rosen

Walter Spaggot

Walter Spaggot, strange old man,
Does things wrong-ways-round,
Like back-to-front or in-side-out,
Or even up-side-down.

He puffs his pipe inside his ear,
Has glasses for his mouth,
And if he wants to travel North
Walks backwards to the South.

He comes from where he never is
And goes to where he's been,
He scrubs his shirt in the bath-tub
And baths in his washing-machine.

Walter Spaggot, strange old man,
Does things wrong-ways-round,
Like back-to-front or in-side-out,
Or even up-side-down.

(Funny old man.)

Peter Wesley-Smith

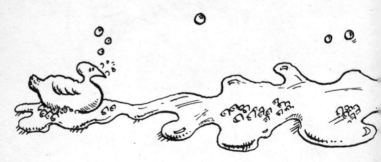

Alone in the Grange

Strange,
Strange,
Is the little old man
Who lives in the Grange.
Old,
Old;
And they say that he keeps
A box full of gold.
Bowed,
Bowed,
Is his thin little back
That once was so proud.
Soft,
Soft,
Are his steps as he climbs
The stairs to the loft.
Black,
Black,
Is the old shuttered house.
Does he sleep on a sack?

They say he does magic,
That he can cast spells,
That he prowls round the garden
Listening for bells;
That he watches for strangers,
Hates every soul,
And peers with his dark eye
Through the keyhole.

I wonder, I wonder,
As I lie in my bed,
Whether he sleeps with his hat on his head?
Is he really magician
With altar of stone,
Or a lonely old gentleman
Left on his own?

Gregory Harrison

Big Gumbo

Great big gawky Gumbo Cole
Couldn't stop growing to save his soul.
Gave up eating, gave up drink,
Sat in the closet, hoped to shrink;
But he grew and grew till he burst the door,
His head went through to the upper floor,
His feet reached down to the cellar door.
He grew still more till the house came down
And Gumbo Cole stepped out on the town
And smashed it in like an old anthill!
Never stopped growing, never will,
Ten times as tall as a telephone pole,
Too big for his breeches – Gumbo Cole!

William Jay Smith

Moses

Moses supposes his toeses are roses,
But Moses supposes erroneously,
For nobody's toeses are poses of roses,
As Moses supposes his toeses to be.

Anon

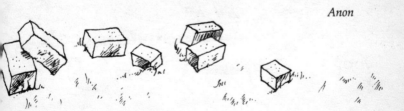

Old Quin Queeribus

Old Quin Queeribus –
  He loved his garden so,
He wouldn't have a rake around,
  A shovel or a hoe.

For each potato's eyes he bought
  Fine spectacles of gold,
And mufflers for the corn, to keep
  Its ears from getting cold.

On every head of lettuce green –
  What do you think of that?
And every head of cabbage, too,
  He tied a garden hat.

Old Quin Queeribus –
  He loved his garden so,
He couldn't eat his growing things,
  He only let them grow!

Nancy Byrd Turner

Mister Beers

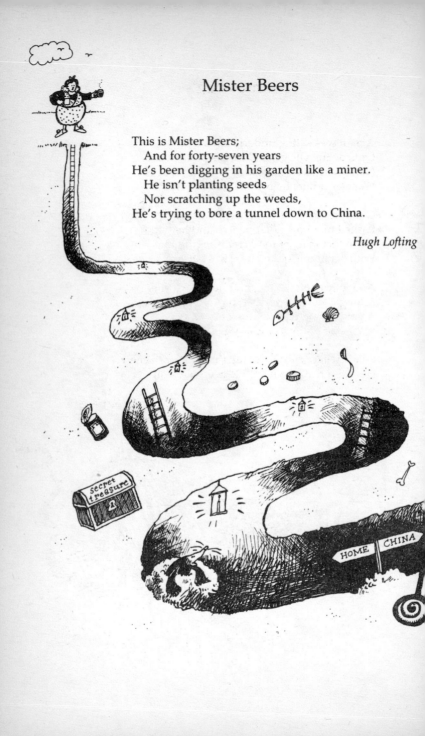

This is Mister Beers;
   And for forty-seven years
He's been digging in his garden like a miner.
   He isn't planting seeds
   Nor scratching up the weeds,
He's trying to bore a tunnel down to China.

Hugh Lofting

Seumas Beg

A man was sitting underneath a tree
Outside the village; and he asked me what
Name was upon this place; and said that he
Was never here before – He told a lot

Of stories to me too. His nose was flat!
I asked him how it happened, and he said
– The first mate of the *Mary Anne* did that
With a marling-spike one day – but he was dead,

And jolly good job too; and he'd have gone
A long way to have killed him – Oh, he had
A gold ring in one ear; the other one
– 'Was bit off by a crocodile, bedad!'

That's what he said. He taught me how to chew!
He was a real nice man. He liked me too!

James Stephens

There Was a Young Farmer of Leeds

There was a young farmer of Leeds
Who swallowed six packets of seeds,
   It soon came to pass
   He was covered with grass,
And he couldn't sit down for the weeds.

Anon

Gulliver in Lilliput

From his nose
Clouds he blows.
When he speaks,
Thunder breaks.
When he eats,
Famine threats.
When he treads,
Mountains' heads
Groan and shake;
Armies quake.
See him stride
Valleys wide,
Over woods,
Over floods.
Troops take heed,
Man and steed:
Left and right,
Speed your flight!
In amaze
Lost I gaze
Toward the skies:
See! and believe your eyes!

Alexander Pope

The Incredible Henry McHugh

I am the Incredible Henry McHugh
you should see the things that I can do!
(and I'm only two)
I can . . .
tie laces in knots
spit peas into pots
squirt all the cream
and scream and SCREAM!

I can . . .
leave toys on the stair
pour honey in hair
scatter fried rice
play football with mice
sit down on the cat
be sick in a hat
slam the door, flood the floor,
and shout 'more, MORE, MORE!'

I can telephone Timbuctoo –
and frequently do,
hurl mud pies and rocks
put jelly in socks
pull Dracula faces
and stick Mum's pins in unlikely places.

I can . . .
pinch, poke, tickle and stroke,
wriggle, giggle, rattle and prattle,
scrawl on the wall
spill paint down the hall
pick heads off the flowers
dribble for hours
and when things go wrong
I just sing my song.

I'M not to blame.
You know my name,
I am Henry McHugh
the INCREDIBLE!
(I'm only two).

Robert Fisher

Jittery Jim

There's room on the bus
For the two of us,
But not for Jittery Jim.

He has a train
And a rocket plane,
He has a seal
That can bark and swim,
And a centipede
With wiggly legs,
And an ostrich
Sitting on ostrich eggs,
And crawfish
Floating in oily kegs!

There's room in the bus
For the two of us,
But we'll shut the door on *him!*

William Jay Smith

Oh Erica, Not Again!

Every time we go on the pier,
  Or down to the sea, that is,
Erica says she is feeling queer
  And it makes her poor head whizz.

Erica says she likes the land,
  And there isn't, alas, much doubt,
As soon as she steps on a trippers' boat
  Erica's legs give out.

Erica's hands will clutch the rail.
  She hears the timbers creak.
She wonders where the lifebelts are –
  Or if we've sprung a leak.

There's never a sign of storm or gale
  But mother's crying 'Quick!'
And so it's just the same old tale,
  Erica's sick!

Max Fatchen

The Young Lady of Twickenham

There was a young lady of Twickenham,
Whose boots were too tight to walk quickenham,
   She bore them awhile,
   But at last, at a stile,
She pulled them both off and was sickenham.

Anon

Thin Flynn

There was once a skeleton named Flynn
Who looked quite remarkably thin,
   All bones, long and white,
   That rattled at night –
He should never have jumped out of his skin!

Anon

Miss T.

It's a very odd thing –
   As odd as can be –
That whatever Miss T. eats
   Turns into Miss T.;
Porridge and apples,
   Mince, muffins, and mutton,
Jam, junket, jumbles –
   Not a rap, not a button
It matters; the moment
   They're out of her plate,
Though shared by Miss Butcher
   And sour Mr Bate;
Tiny and cheerful,
   And neat as can be,
Whatever Miss T. eats
Turns into Miss T.

Walter de la Mare

The Young Girl in the Choir

There was a young girl in the choir,
Whose voice rose hoir and hoir,
   Till it reached such a height,
   It was clear out of sight,
And they found it next day on the spoir.

Anon

The Old Fellow from Tyre

There was an old fellow of Tyre,
Who constantly sat on the fire.
   When asked, 'Are you hot?'
   He said, 'Certainly not.
I'm James Winterbotham, Esquire.'

Anon

Tommy

Young Tommy would not go to bed,
But sat watching TV instead,
  As he stayed up to stare
  His face went all square
And aerials grew from his head.

Anon

You Are Old, Father William

'You are old, Father William,' the young man said,
  'And your hair has become very white;
And yet you incessantly stand on your head –
  Do you think, at your age, it is right?'

'In my youth,' Father William replied to his son,
  'I feared it might injure the brain;
But, now that I'm perfectly sure I have none,
  Why, I do it again and again.'

'You are old,' said the youth, 'as I mentioned before,
  And have grown most uncommonly fat;
Yet you turned a back-somersault in at the door –
  Pray, what is the reason for that?'

'In my youth,' said the sage, as he shook his grey locks,
  'I kept all my limbs very supple
By the use of this ointment – one shilling the box –
  Allow me to sell you a couple?'

'You are old,' said the youth, 'and your jaws are too weak
  For anything tougher than suet;
Yet you finished the goose, with the bones and the beak –
  Pray, how did you manage to do it?'

'In my youth,' said his father, 'I took to the law,
  And argued each case with my wife;
And the muscular strength, which it gave to my jaw,
  Has lasted the rest of my life.'

'You are old,' said the youth, 'one would hardly suppose
    That your eye was as steady as ever;
Yet you balanced an eel on the end of your nose –
    What made you so awfully clever?'

'I have answered three questions, and that is enough,'
    Said his father. 'Don't give yourself airs!
Do you think I can listen all day to such stuff?
    Be off, or I'll·kick you downstairs!'

Lewis Carroll

The Man on the Flying Trapeze

Sporting and capering high in the breeze,
cavorting about from trapeze to trapeze
is an aerial acrobat, slim as a ribbon,
as daring and free as a tree-swinging gibbon.

He hangs by his fingers, his toes and his knees,
he dangles and dips with astonishing ease,
then springs into space as though racing on wings,
gliding between his precarious swings.

He cheerfully executes perilous plunges,
dangerous dives, unforgettable lunges,
delicate scoops and spectacular swoops,
breathtaking triple flips, hazardous loops.

Then this midair magician with nerves made of steel
somersaults, catches and hangs by one heel.
As the audience roars for the king of trapezes
he takes out his handkerchief, waves it . . . and sneezes.

Balanced above us, the high wire king
skips with a swivel, a sway and a swing.
He dances, he prances, he leaps through the air,
then hangs by his teeth while he's combing his hair.
He seems not to notice the perilous height
as he stands on his left hand and waves with his right.

Jack Prelutsky

Be Quiet!

The world's greatest snorer
  Was Barrington Brown.
His snores shook the windows
  And rattled the town.

The people grew frantic
  And fearful with fright,
And cried to each other,
  'What happens tonight?'

They lullabyed softly
  But who could ignore
The deafening noise
  Of that terrible snore?

They tied up their heads
  And their eardrums they bound,
But nothing could soften
  That thundering sound.

They made a giant clothes-peg
  And placed on his nose.
With one mighty snore
  Like a rocket it rose.

So they all left the town
  In their cars and their carts,
'We must be away
  Before Barrington starts.'

Then Barrington woke,
  'Where's everyone gone?'
And then he turned over
And went snoring on!

Max Fatchen

The Pessimist

Nothing to do but work,
   Nothing to eat but food,
Nothing to wear but clothes
   To keep one from going nude.

Nothing to breathe but air,
   Quick as a flash 'tis gone;
Nowhere to fall but off,
   Nowhere to stand but on.

Nothing to comb but hair,
   Nowhere to sleep but in bed,
Nothing to weep but tears,
   Nothing to bury but dead.

Nothing to sing but songs,
   Ah, well, alas! alack!
Nowhere to go but out,
   Nowhere to come but back.

Nothing to see but sights,
   Nothing to quench but thirst,
Nothing to have but what we've got;
   Thus thro' life we are cursed.

Nothing to strike but a gait;
   Everything moves that goes.
Nothing at all but common sense
   Can ever withstand these woes.

Ben King

The Optimist (1)

Somebody said that it couldn't be done,
But he, with a grin replied,
He'd never be one to say it couldn't be done –
Leastways, not till he'd tried.
So he buckled right in with a trace of a grin,
By golly he went right to it.
He tackled The Thing That Couldn't Be Done!
And he couldn't do it.

Anon

The Optimist (2)

The optimist fell ten storeys
   And at each window bar
He shouted to the folks inside:
   'Doing all right so far!'

Anon

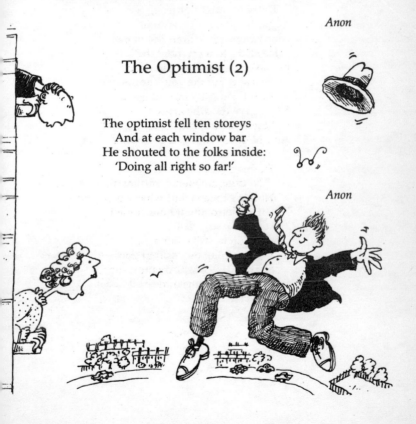

Old Mrs Thing-um-e-bob

Old Mrs Thing-um-e-bob,
  Lives at you-know-where.
Dropped her what-you-may-call-it down
  The well of the kitchen stair.

'Gracious me!' said Thing-um-e-bob,
  'This don't look too bright.
I'll ask old Mr What's-his-name
  To try to put it right.'

Along came Mr What's-his-name,
  He said, 'You've broke the lot!
I'll have to see what I can do
  With some of the you-know-what.'

So he gave the what-you-may-call-it a pit
  And he gave it a bit of a pat,
And he put it all together again
  With a little of this and that.

And he gave the what-you-may-call-it a dib
  And he gave it a dab as well
When all of a sudden he heard a note
  As clear as any bell.

'It's as good as new!' cried What's-his-name.
  'But please remember, now,
In future Mrs Thing-um-e-bob
  You'll have to go you-know-how.'

Charles Causley

My Name Is . . .

My name is Sluggery-wuggery
My name is Worms-for-tea
My name is Swallow-the-table-leg
My name is Drink-the-Sea.

My name is I-eat-saucepans
My name is I-like-snails
My name is Grand-piano-George
My name is I-ride-whales.

My name is Jump-the-chimney
My name is Bite-my-knee
My name is Jiggery-pokery
And Riddle-me-ree, and ME.

Pauline Clarke

Doctor Bell

Doctor Bell fell down the well
And broke his collar-bone.
Doctors should attend the sick
And leave the well alone.

Anon

There Was a Man

There was a man whose nose was long
and bent like some old kitchen tap
but he just laughed and sang this song,
a merry and contented chap.

'I know my nose is long, my nose,
but I don't mind one little bit,
and this because I must suppose
I cannot see the end of it.

I wouldn't worry if my eyes
came out on stalks, or saw behind,
or swivelled round like eyes of flies,
my friends, I really wouldn't mind.

Nor if I had a donkey's ears
or pinky ones on baby mice,
it wouldn't bring me any tears,
I think it would be rather nice.

For if your nose is long as mine,
there's nothing much that you can do,
and, anyway, I'm feeling fine,
I hope that you, my dear, are, too.

I know my nose is long, my nose,
I keep on singing it out loud,
I'm never shy of friends or foes,
I like myself, I do, I'm proud.

Be happy then with what you are,
whether your nose is long or bent,
For every leaf and every star
is wonderful and different.'

Leonard Clark

Cousin Reggie

Cousin Reggie
who adores the sea
lives in the Midlands
unfortunately.

He surfs down escalators
in department stores
and swims the High Street
on all of his fours.

Sunbathes on the pavement
paddles in the gutter
(I think our Reggie's
a bit of a nutter).

Roger McGough

The Young Man who Couldn't See Why

There was a young man who asked, 'Why
Can't I look in my ear with my eye?
  If I put my mind to it
  I'm sure I could do it.
You never can tell till you try!'

Anon

Cavendish McKellar

Cavendish McKellar,
Clever little feller,
Bought himself a new umbrella,
Rubber boots and new galoshes,
Plastic hats and mackintoshes –
All to stop his mother's grizzles
When he frolicked in the drizzles.

Alas, his troubles were in vain.
But why?
        It didn't rain.

Peter Wesley-Smith

Granny

Through every nook and every cranny
The wind blew in on poor old Granny;
Around her knees, into each ear
(And up her nose as well, I fear).

All through the night the wind grew worse,
It nearly made the vicar curse.
The top had fallen off the steeple
Just missing him (and other people).

It blew on man; it blew on beast.
It blew on nun; it blew on priest.
It blew the wig off Auntie Fanny –
But most of all, it blew on Granny!

Spike Milligan

Burglar Bill

Forth from his den to steal he stole,
His bags of chink he chunk,
And many a wicked smile he smole,
And many a wink he wunk.

Anon

Index of First Lines

Index of Authors